Santa's First Helper

SANTA'S FIRST HELPER

Written by
Gerald M. Hoppe

Illustrated by
Anne M. Hickman and Gerald M. Hoppe

VANTAGE PRESS
New York / Atlanta
Los Angeles / Chicago

FIRST EDITION

Published by Vantage Press, Inc.
516 West 34th Street, New York, New York 10001

Manufactured in the United States of America
ISBN: 0-533-07493-2

To Marc E. Hoppe
with love and hope

Acknowledgments

The author would like to give thanks to the members of his family and friends who have supported and encouraged this work. He would also like to thank the many children he saw when he served as a Santa's helper in Syracuse, New York, for the past several years.

One final and special thank-you goes to John J. Sweeney for his assistance and suggestions.

Santa's First Helper

Once upon a time, way back when, far, far, up in the north country where the winds are chilling cold and it always snows, there is a place called the North Pole, where a well-known fellow named Santa Claus lives.

W ell, it was two days before Christmas, this particular year. Santa Claus was very busy as he scurried around checking on last minute details, making sure every toy and gift was ready to be delivered on Christmas Eve.

He went to meet with the head elf, WeeOne, to check on the condition of the reindeer and the scheduling of the loading of the sleigh. WeeOne said, "Don't worry, Santa. Everything is on schedule and the reindeer are doing just fine. I personally will go over every final detail so you can relax and get your rest."

shop,
ery year
elp with
ed to do
to peek
kings, to
t Santa.
the chil-

on that night of De-
to his large, soft, warm
sleep to give him extra

Meanwhile, back in the
WeeOne was dreaming his yearly dream
he went with Santa on his magical trip
the reindeer and sleigh, but WeeOne w
more. He wanted to be Santa! He war
in on all the boys and girls, to fill the s
enjoy some of the surprise snacks the
You see, he wanted to be the one to m
dren happy at Christmas time.

$\mathbf{Y}$es, WeeOne wanted to be Santa, well, to be like him and have his powers anyway. But where did the magic powers come from? It couldn't be Santa's red suit, because WeeOne knew Santa had several that he wore. It couldn't be the reindeer or the sleigh, because once in a while there wasn't

enough room on the rooftop for the reindeer and sleigh to land, but Santa would still glide up to the chimney by himself. WeeOne thought and thought. "Why, it must be Santa's long white beard, because Santa always has that!" decided WeeOne.

"Well then, while Santa is sleeping, I must go and cut off his beard. Then I'll use his magical white hair to make a magical beard for myself." He crept into Santa's open bedroom window

and carefully stepped over the squeaky floorboard. Clip! Clip! Clip! It seemed to take an eternity as WeeOne nervously collected a whole bag of curly white hair from the sleeping Santa.

Back out the window went WeeOne, back to the toy shop. *Let's see,* thought WeeOne. *I'll use some elastic and some white cloth and some thread and a needle.* He worked well into the night, and when he was done, a swell-looking beard had been fashioned. "Now, this will surely do just fine." WeeOne beamed, his face lighting up with a big smile.

WeeOne quietly went out to the stables and woke up Donner. As he hooked him up to a small cart that one reindeer could handle, WeeOne remembered what Santa always did to get going. He closed his eyes and imagined what it would feel like to fly through the air. Then he put his finger up to his nose and wiggled it. He did it again! Nothing happened! He didn't move. "Oh, no," sighed WeeOne as he slowly and sadly realized that the magic didn't come from Santa's hair.

Early Christmas Eve morning, Santa began to stir as he rubbed his eyes and his chin. Then he let out a scream. "Mama, what happened? What happened to my beard and my hair? Mama!" Before Mrs. Claus could get up the stairs, WeeOne was at the door with tears in his eyes. As he handed Santa back his beard all sewed and full of elastic, he apologized and explained why he had done such a silly thing.

14

Santa wiped away a tear from his friend's face. "WeeOne, I'll forgive you, but why didn't you tell me about your dream? What you did was very wrong, even though you wanted something good to happen from it. My magic comes from the Spirit of Christmas itself! Nobody can take that away!" Santa continued, "We have a very big problem now. My beard will grow back, but not by tonight. None of the moms or dads who don't have chimneys, who have to let me in the door, will recognize me. They might not let me in."

"Well," WeeOne said, "there's always my fake one. Since it's yours anyway, you might as well have it back."

So Santa wore the beard WeeOne had made, so the moms and dads could recognize him. In fact, he kind of enjoyed being able to slip off the beard for a second now and then to eat a gooey cookie left for him. His beard stayed a lot cleaner this way, too.

Santa made a big decision that early Christmas. "I don't have to have a real beard all the time. I can use a pretend one sometimes. I will still look nice."

To this very day then, because of WeeOne's dream and what he did to Santa, no little boy or girl who sits on Santa's lap will ever know for sure if it's the true Santa or not. He doesn't need to have a beard of his own anymore.

Oh, and by the way, WeeOne, because of his honesty, was put in charge of getting Santa's helpers into the stores before Christmas so they could hear what the children wanted Santa to bring them on Christmas Eve. Now, Santa and his helpers could choose to grow their own beards or wear pretend ones.

Do you know which Santa is the real one?

MERRY CHRISTMAS